A New House for Clarence

Written by Michèle Dufresne

Illustrated by Max Stasiuk

CONTENTS

PIONEER VALLEY EDUCATIONAL PRESS, INC.

CHAPTER 1
A Tiny House

One day, the doorbell rang.
Clarence went to the door
and opened it.
It was Lily at the door.
She was holding a basket.

"Good morning, Clarence," said Lily.
"I baked some muffins."

"Muffins, yum!" said Clarence.
"Come in. We can have muffins
and tea!"

3

Lily went into Clarence's house.
She put the basket of muffins
on the table.
She looked around
for a place to sit.
There was something
on every chair.

On one chair,
there were magazines.
On another chair,
there were books.
On another chair,
there was a big, stuffed teddy bear.
There was nowhere for Lily to sit.

Clarence pushed some books
off a chair and onto the floor.
"You can sit here," he said.
"I will make some tea."

Clarence took a small kettle
and filled it with water.
Then he put the kettle
on a very tiny stove.

"Clarence, I think you need
a bigger house," said Lily.
"This house is too small
for you. You are not
a little dragon anymore.
Now you are a big dragon.
You need a bigger house.
A house for a big dragon."

Clarence looked around
at his house.
He looked at all the things
on all his chairs.
He looked at his little bed
and his little kitchen.
"Yes, I do need a bigger house,"
Clarence said. "Can you help me
find a bigger one?"

"Yes! Let's go look today!" said Lily.

CHAPTER 2
A Bigger House

After they ate the muffins,
Clarence and Lily went to look
for a new house.

"Let's look in the forest,"
said Lily. "We can find
a nice big house in the forest."

Lily and Clarence walked
and walked looking
for a new house.

"Look," said Lily.
"Here is a house in the ground."

Clarence looked at the house.
"That's not a good house
for me," he said.
"That's a good house for a fox."

"Look," said Lily.
"There is a house in a tree."

Clarence looked at the house
in the tree.
"That's not a good house
for me," he said.
"That's a good house
for a squirrel."

"Look, Clarence," said Lily.
"Look at this big house
under the bridge."

Clarence looked at the house.
"That's not a good house
for me," he said.
"That's a good house
for a troll!"

"Grrr," said the troll.

"Oh, yes. This is a good house for a troll," said Lily.

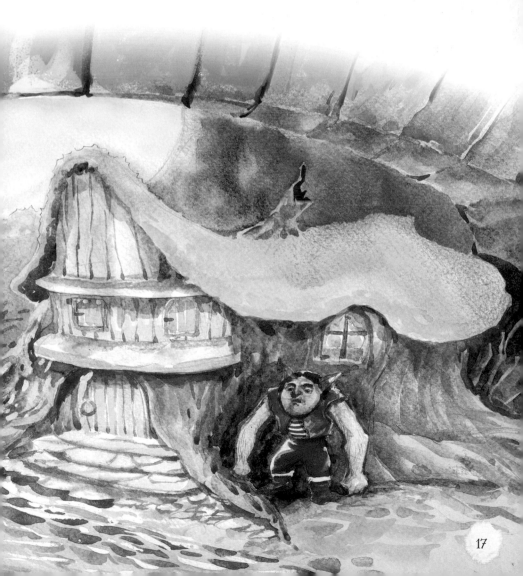

Lily and Clarence walked
and walked. Then they came
to a big cave with a door.

"Look at this house," said Lily.
"This house looks big."

"Let's look inside," said Clarence.

Lily and Clarence
went into the house.
There was a big bed.
There was a big table
and a lot of chairs to sit on.

"Look," said Lily.
"Look at the nice fireplace.
We can sit by the fireplace
on cold winter days."

"This is a good house for me,"
said Clarence.
"I'm moving in!"